FUNNY JOKES

FOR

FUNNY KIDS

WITH HAND DRAWN

cartoons!

by JIMMY JONES

Over 370 Really Funny Jokes For Kids!

CONTENTS

Funny Jokes For Kids!

Q: What do you call a dinosaur who is going to have a baby next week?

A: A Preggosaurus!

Q: Why did the giant squid eat six ships that were carrying potatoes?

A: Nobody can only eat one potato ship!

Q: Why did the gorilla have huge nostrils?

A: She had big fingers!

Q: Why was the fish sad about his report card?

A: His grades were all under "C"!

Q: Why are tennis players so loud?

A: They always raise a racquet!

Q: Why was the oak tree at the dentist?

A: It was having a root canal!

Q: What fruit do vampires love?

A: Necktarines!

Q: What do you call a witch who lives near the beach?

A: A sandwitch!

Q: Why was the didgeridoo at the office?

A: To answer the phone if the boomerang!

Q: Why did the man have so much facial hair?

A: It seemed to just grow on him!

Q: What do you call the archaeologist who works for the English Police?
A: Sherlock Bones!

Q: Which nails do carpenters try not to hit?
A: Fingernails!

Q: What has 40 legs but can't walk?
A: Half a centipede!

Q: What would Superman be called if he lost all his super powers?
A: Man!

Q: What is 186 feet tall and made from cheese and pepperoni?

A: The leaning tower of Pizza!

Q: What do birds send out at Halloween?

A: Tweets!!

Q: Which musical instrument is in your bathroom?

A: The tuba toothpaste!

Q: If a deer costs one dollar, what is it?

A: A buck!

Q: Who carries a basket, is scared of wolves and says bad words?

A: Little Rude Riding Hood!

Q: What happens when 2 silkworms have a race?

A: It ends in a tie!

Q: What do you call a man who lives in the toilet?

A: John!

Q: What do you call a boy named Lee sitting by himself?

A: Lonely! (Lone Lee)

Q: Why did the toilet paper roll down the steep hill?

A: He wanted to get to the bottom!

Q: What is an alligator's favorite sports drink?

A: GatorAde!

Q: Why did Cinderella leave the basketball team?

A: She always ran away from the ball!

Q: What did the cloud wear underneath
his raincoat?

A: Thunderpants!

Q: Why did the whale get dressed in his best clothes?

A: He was going to the Orca-stra!

Q: Why did the snowman wear a bow tie?

A: To go to the snowball!

Q: What do elves love learning the most at school?"

A: The elf-abet!

Q: What did the farmer call his cow that was twitching and twitching?

A: Beef Jerky!

Q: Where did the car go for a morning swim?

A: The carpool!

Q: Why do vampires take so much cough medicine?

A: To stop their coffin!

Q: What did the baby light bulb say to her mommy?

A: I wuv you watts!

Q: If a freezing cold dog sits on a bunny, what is it?

A: A chili dog on a bun!

Q: Why was it easy for Thomas Edison to invent the light bulb?

A: He was really, really bright!

Q: What was the Monster's favorite type of cheese?

A: Monsterella!

Q: How can a car be like a frog?

A: If it is being toad!

Q: What did one coin say to the other coin?

A: Together, we make cents!

Q: What do you call the dinosaur that had a car accident?

A: The Tyrannosauraus wreck!

Q: What did the grape say when the man stepped on it?

A: Not much, it just let out a little wine!

Q: What do you get treated for if a computer has bitten you?

A: A Megabyte!

Q: Why did the sheep get a ticket from the policeman?

A: She made an illegal ewe turn!

Q: What did the dad potato name his son?

A: Chip!

Q: There were 4 cats on a chair and one jumped off. How many were left?

A: None, because they were copycats!

Q: What is white and black and eats like a horse?

A: A zebra!

Q: Why did the boy stand on a cow?

A: To be a cowboy!

Q: What is orange, grows in the ground and sounds like a parrot?

A: A carrot!

Q: What do you call an adult bear that has no teeth?

A: The gummy bear!

Q: Why did the fish live in salt water?

A: Pepper made him sneeze!

Q: What fish would never bite a woman?

A: A man eating shark!

Q: What is worse than finding a worm when you are eating an apple?
A: Finding half the worm!

Q: Why did the mushroom take dance lessons?
A: He was a fungi (fun guy)!

Q: Why did he have to quit dance lessons?
A: There wasn't mush room!

Q: What do you call a toy that does nothing all day long?
A: An inaction figure!

Funnier Kids Jokes!

Q: What do you call a snake that has no clothes on?

A: Snaked!

Q: Why was the glow worm looking sad?

A: His kids weren't very bright!

Q: How do you fit lots more pigs on your farm?

A: Build a huge sty-scraper!

Q: What goes up and then down but doesn't actually move?

A: Stairs!

Q: If the cheese isn't your cheese, what sort of cheese is it?

A: Nacho cheese!

Q: Why was the Egyptian boy so sad?

A: His dad was a mummy!

Q: What do you call a boy floating in the sea with no arms, no legs and no body – just a head?

A: Bob!

Q: How can you cut a wave in half?

A: With a sea saw!

Q: What should you give a pig who has a rash?

A: Some oinkment!

Q: Why do basketball players love babies so much?

A: Because they both dribble!

Q: Why did the vampire get in big trouble at the blood bank?

A: He was drinking on the job!

Q: Why didn't the bear wear shoes to school?

A: He liked to have bear feet!

Q: What did the picture say to the window?

A: Help! I've been framed!

Q: What do you call a girl with one
really short leg?
A: Eileen! (I lean)

Q: What did the judge wear to work?
A: His lawsuit!

Q: What do you call the bunny that comes 3 days after Easter?

A: Choco Late!

Q: What do you call a lady on a tennis court?

A: Annette! (A net!)

Q: What do you call a pig that can do kung fu?

A: A pork chop!

Q: What do dogs love to eat for breakfast?

A: Pooched eggs!

Q: What would you have if a chicken laid an egg on top of a barn roof?

A: An eggroll!

Q: What is the easiest way to count 273 cows?

A: Use a cowculator!

Q: When it gets really cold what does an octopus wear?

A: His coat of arms!

Q: Why did the elephant decide to leave the circus?

A: He was sick and tired of working for peanuts!

Q: What sound can you hear when a train is eating?

A: Chew chew!

Q: What do you call a dog who has a fever?

A: A hot dog!

Q: If a boomerang doesn't come back, what is it?

A: A stick!

Q: What kind of fish did King Arthur eat every Saturday night?

A: Swordfish!

Q: Why sound do you hear if a pterodactyl uses your toilet?

A: Nothing because the "P" is silent!

Q: Why did the dog make friends with the tree?

A: He liked its bark!

Q: Where do sheep like to go for vacations?

A: The baaaahamas!

Q: What do you call a dinosaur with really bad eyesight?

A: A DoYouThinkTheySaurUs!

Q: Why was the broom late for work at the factory?

A: He overswept!

Q: What does a frog like to drink with his dinner?

A: Croak-a-cola!

Q: What do you get if an elephant stands on the roof of your house?

A: Mushed rooms!

Q: Why wouldn't the oyster share her pearls?

A: She was a little shellfish!

Q: Why are ghosts no good at lying?

A: You can usually see right through them!

Q: Which bird should wear a wig?

A: The bald eagle!

Q: What did the baby corn ask his mother?

A: Where is pop corn?

Q: Why did the judge sentence the fish to 3 years in jail?

A: He was Gill Ty!

Q: What do clocks do every day after lunch?

A: They go back four seconds!

Q: What kind of cat is no fun to play a game with?

A: The cheetah!

Q: What kind of sandwich did the shark order for his lunch?

A: Peanut butter and jellyfish!

Q: What did the crab take when it was sick?

A: Vitamin sea!

Q: What is a royal pardon?

A: What the queen decrees after she burps!

Q: Where did the mouse park his row boat?

A: The hickory dickory dock!

Q: What did the lawyer say as the skunk walked into the courtroom?

A: Odor in the court!

Q: Why did the football coach go to the bank before the big game?

A: To get his quarterback!

Q: Why did the boy put peanut butter on the busy road?

A: It went with the traffic jam!

Q: What do you call an alligator that robbed the bank?

A: A crookodile!

Laugh Out Loud Jokes For Kids!

Q: What did the mailman do when he found out the mailbox was broken?

A: He stamped his feet!

Q: What do you call a mother cow that gave birth to her calf?

A: DeCalfinated!

Q: Why did the pony stop singing in the farm band?

A: She was a little hoarse!

Q: What do you call a boy with 3 rabbits in his pockets?

A: Warren!

Q: How did the Vikings send a secret message?

A: Norse code!

Q: Which part of the eye always does the most work?

A: The pupil!

Q: Why did the cow eat all your grass?

A: It was a lawn moo-er!

Q: What washes up on the smallest beach in the world?

A: Microwaves!

Q: What is an Oak tree's favorite cold drink?

A: Root beer!

Q: What do you give a lemon that has hurt itself?

A: Lemonade!

Q: Why did the photo end up in jail?

A: It was framed!

Q: What did the boxer drink just before the big fight?

A: Fruit punch!

Q: Where do the friendly horses live?

A: In your neigh-borhood!

Q: How did the butcher introduce his new girlfriend to his family?

A: Meet Patty!

Q: Why did the boy put 3 pieces of candy under his pillow?

A: So he could have sweet dreams!

Q: What is the worst type of jam in the world?

A: A traffic jam!

Q: Which type of fish swims at night?

A: A starfish!

Q: Who's in charge of the cornfield?

A: The kernel!

Q: What is small, round, white, lives in a jar and giggles?

A: A tickled onion!

Q: Why did Johnny bring a ladder to his school?

A: So he could go to high school!

Q: What kind of horses go outside when it's dark?

A: Nightmares!

Q: Why can milk move so fast?

A: It's pasteurised before you even see it!

Q: What happens if there is a fight in the fish and chip shop?

A: The fish get battered!

Q: What sport do horses love?

A: Stable tennis!

Q: What are two rows of vegetables called?

A: A dual cabbage way!

Q: What did the lawyers say to the dentist?

A: Make sure you tell the tooth, the whole tooth and nothing but the tooth?

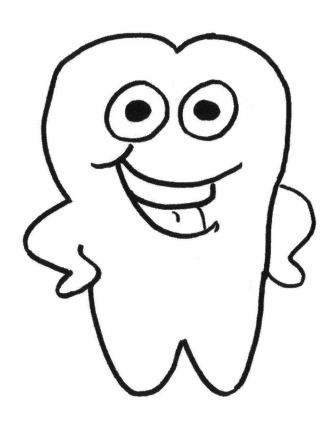

Q: Why do golfers wear 3 pairs of pants?

A: In case they get a hole in one!

Q: Why did the girl take her ruler to bed?

A: To see how long she slept!

Q: Why did the grape go to the ball with the prune?

A: He couldn't get a date!

Q: What is the easiest way to make a hot dog stand?

A: Steal its chair!

Q: Why did the banana end up in hospital?

A: It wasn't peeling very well!

Q: Why did the secret agent stay in bed all day?

A: He was under cover!

Q: What did one tomato say to the other tomato in the tomato race?

A: Ketchup!

Q: Why are fish really clever?

A: They live in schools!

Q: What did the scrambled egg say to the whisk?

A: Stop beating me!

Q: Why did the milking stool have three legs?

A: The cow's got the udder!

Q: Which desert is no fun to eat?

A: Apple Grumble!

Q: Why don't teddy bears eat much for lunch?

A: They are always stuffed!

Q: How do prisoners in jail talk to their friends?

A: On their **cell phones!**

Q: What do you call 5 security guards at the Samsung shop?

A: Guardians of the Galaxy!

Q: Why are computers tired when they get home from work?

A: They had a hard drive!

Q: What is the name of the movie about a broken pencil?

A: Pointless!

Q: Why did the artist never win at any sports?

A: He kept on drawing!

Q: Why was the cucumber so embarrassed?

A: She saw the salad dressing!

Q: Which country do sharks love to visit?

A: Finland!

Q: What has four wheels, weighs 10 tons and flies?

A: A garbage truck!

Q: What is a light-year?

A: Like a normal year, but doesn't weigh very much!

Q: Which animal appears on legal documents?

A: A seal!

Q: What is the best school so you can learn how to greet people?

A: Hi school!

Q: How did the dog stop the video from playing?

A: By pressing the paws button!

Q: Which city building usually has the most stories?

A: The library!

Hilarious Kids Jokes!

Q: Where did the pencil go for his vacation?

A: Pencil Vania!

Q: Why did the farmer drive a steam roller through his field?

A: He wanted to grow mashed potatoes!

Q: Why did the 3 scientists get rid of their doorbell?

A: So they could win the no-bell prize!

Q: Which state has really small cans of soft drink?

A: Mini Soda!

Q: Why doesn't Peter Pan ever stop flying?

A: e Neverlands!

Q: How can you learn how to make a banana split?

A: Go to sundae school!

Q: What happens if you cross a fish with an elephant?

A: You get swimming trunks!

Q: What do nuts say if they catch a cold?

A: Cashew!

Q: What do you call a lawyer's daughter?

A: Sue!

Q: What sort of dog really loves bubble baths?

A: Shampoodles!

Q: Why did the man run around and around his bed 4 times?

A: To catch up on some sleep!

Q: What do you call 28 rabbits walking in a row backwards?

A: A receding hareline!

Q: How did the cook fix the broken vegetable?

A: He used tomato paste!

Q: Why was the alligator using a magnifying glass?

A: He was an investigator!

Q: Where did the turtle stop to get a snack?

A: The shell station!

Q: Why did the bacteria travel across the microscope?

A: So he could get to the other slide!

Q: When the buffalo was leaving to go to work, what did he say to his son?

A: Bison! (bye son!)

Q: What do you call a cow in a washing machine?

A: A milkshake!

Q: What did the teeth say to the gums?

A: The dentist is taking us out tonight!

Q: Why do bananas put on so much sunscreen at the beach?

A: Otherwise they might peel!

Q: If you lend money to a bison, what is it?

A: A Buff A Loan!

Q: Why was the basketball court really slippery?

A: The players love to dribble!

Q: Why did the raspberry call 911?

A: She was in a jam!

Q: What do you call a pig with no personality?

A: A boar!

64

Q: Why did the man have to leave the car assembly line?

A: He took too many brakes!

Q: What do you hear after 2 porcupines have a kiss?

A: Ouch!

Q: Why is a guitar opposite to a fish??

A: A guitar can be tuned but you can't tuna fish!

Q: Why was it so hot at the basketball game?

A: Most of the fans had left!

Q: Why is it no fun to play cards in Africa?

A: Too many cheetahs!

Q: If you are really cold and grumpy what do you eat?

A: A brrrgrrr!

Q: What do you call a number that keeps moving around and around?
A: A roamin' numeral!

Q: What do you call a fly that has lost its wings?
A: A walk!

Q: What stays in the corner and but then travels all over the country?

A: A stamp!

Q: Why did the bird book into the hospital?

A: To get some tweetment!

Q: How do you know when the moon is about to go bankrupt?

A: When it's down to a quarter!

Q: Why do birds fly north in springtime?

A: It's way too far to walk!

68

Q: Where do cows go on their day off?

A: The Mooseum!

Q: Why was the computer sneezing all day?

A: It had a really bad virus!

Q: Why couldn't the cross eyed teacher get a job?

A: She couldn't control her pupils!

Q: What would you call it if worms took over the entire world?

A: Global Worming!

Q: What do you call a hippo with a messy room?

A: A Hippopota Mess!

Q: Where do hamsters go for their vacation?

A: Hamsterdam!

Q: If a cow and a duck got married, what would you have?
A: Milk and quackers!

Q: What's another name for two banana peels?
A: Slippers!

Q: Why did the belt go to jail for 3 years?

A: He was caught holding up a pair of pants!

Q: Why was the computer feeling so cold?

A: It's Windows were left open!

Q: Why did the lamb go to the mall?

A: To go to the baaaaarber shop!

Q: If a plumber married a ballerina, what would their child do?

A: Become a tap dancer!

Q: What do you call a belt with a built in watch?

A: A waist of time!

Q: Why did the elephant run away from the computer?

A: She was scared of the mouse!

Q: Why do zebras like to watch really old movies?

A: They are in black and white!

Even Funnier Jokes For Kids!

Q: What do you call a fairy who hasn't had a shower for 3 weeks?

A: Stinker Bell!

Q: What did the old tornado say to his wife?

A: Let's twist again! Like we did last summer!

Q: Why did the racehorse go to McDonalds?

A: He wanted some fast food!

Q: Why did the window go to the hospital?

A: It had panes!

Q: What's a fortune teller's favorite type of tree?

A: Palms!

Q: Where do monkeys do their exercise?
A: The jungle gym!

Q: How much does it cost a pirate to buy corn?
A: A buccaneer!

Q: Why did the computer let out a tiny squeak?

A: Someone stepped on its mouse!

Q: Why was the rabbit scared of the comb?

A: He heard it was always teasing hares!

Q: Why was the computer feeling old?

A: It was losing its memory!

Q: Why do mice take really long showers?

A: They like to feel squeaky clean!

Q: What did the vampire get when he bit the snowman?

A: Frostbite!

Q: What do you use to wrap a cloud?

A: A rainbow!

Q: Why were the ghosts hired as cheerleaders?

A: They had so much spirit!

Q: Where did the really cool mouse live?

A: In his mousepad!

Q: What can you use to open the great lakes?

A: The Florida Keys!

Q: What do you call a pig that was caught speeding?

A: A road hog!

Q: How did the fish know how much he weighed?

A: He used his scales!

Q: Why did the musician go to the bakery?

A: To buy a drumroll!

Q: What happens if you throw some butter out the window?
A: You see a butterfly!

Q: What song does Tarzan love at Christmas?
A: Jungle Bells!

Q: How do bees get smarter?
A: They have a spelling bee!

Q: What happened when the elephant ate a computer?
A: He had lots of memory!

Q: What did the number 0 say to his friend, number 8?

A: Nice belt!

Q: Why do owls love going to parties?
A: They are always such a hoot!

Q: Why did the pirate stop playing cards?
A: He was sitting on the deck!

Q: What is the best day to go to the pool?
A: Sunday!

Q: Why did the chef spend 10 years in jail?
A: He beat the eggs and whipped the cream!

Q: Why was the boy standing on a clock?

A: He wanted to be on time!

Q: Why was the snake crossing the busy road?

A: To get to the other sssssside!

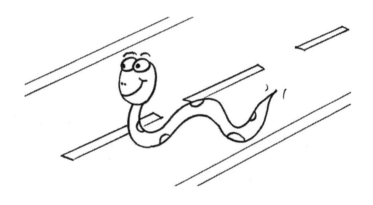

Q: If you're American in the kitchen, what are you in the toilet?

A: Euro Peein!

Q: What did the cat say when the boy stepped on its tail?

A: Me-ow!

Q: What happened to the cat that ate 3 lemons?

A: It became a sour puss!

Q: Who is the master of the pencil case?

A: The ruler!

Q: Why didn't the sun bother going to university?

A: It already had six thousand degrees!

Q: What do you call the girl who has a frog on her head?

A: Lily!

Q: How do hair stylists do haircuts faster?

A: They take short cuts!

Q: What did the snowman eat for his breakfast?

A: Frosted Flakes!

Q: How can you make friends with a squirrel?

A: Climb up a tree and act like a nut!

Q: What kind of underwear did the reporter wear on TV?

A: News briefs!

Q: Why was the dog like a telephone?

A: It had a collar I.D.!

Q: Why did the chicken go for a jog?

A: She needed the egg-cersize!

Q: Why did the cow wear a bell on the way to the farm?

A: Her horn didn't work!

Q: What has one head, four legs but only one foot?

A: A Bed!

Q: What did the taxi driver say when he couldn't find his taxi?

A: Where is my taxi?

Q: Why did the shoemaker go straight to heaven?

A: He had a good sole!

Q: What did the big cow say to the small cow?

A: Moooooove over!

Q: What did the carrot and the tomato say to the celery?

A: Quit stalking us!

Q: Why did the boy laugh after his time in hospital?

A: The doctor had him in stitches!

Q: Why did the math teacher wear dark sunglasses?

A: His pupils were too bright!

Silly Jokes For Kids!

Q: If a king was only 12 inches tall, what would you call him?

A: A ruler!

Q: What vegetables do sailors try to avoid?

A: Leeks!

Q: What did the egg in a hurry say to the other egg?

A: Let's get cracking!

Q: Why did the match have to quit playing baseball?

A: One strike and he would be out!

Q: What sort of music do planets love to sing?

A: Neptunes!

Q: What did the big wall say to the smaller wall?

A: Let's catch up at the corner!

Q: If you put a snake and a pie into a magician's hat, what would you have?

A: A pie-thon!

Q: If a monkey exploded, what sound would it make?

A: Baboom!

Q: What happened to the turkey who started boxing?

A: The stuffing was knocked out of him!

Q: Why should you never tell a joke while standing on ice?

A: It might crack up!

Q: What starts with gas but only has 3 letters?

A: A car!

Q: Why was the cat really scared of the tree?

A: Because of its bark!

Q: Why was the math book sad and grumpy?

A: It had so many problems!

Q: Where is the biggest pencil factory in the United States?

A: Pennsylvania!

Q: What was the fake noodle's Secret Agent name?

A: The Impasta!

Q: Why did the bee's hair stick together?

A: She used a honeycomb!

Q: What did the lion say when it first met the gazelle?

A: Pleased to eat you!

Q: What do you call a bruise on a T-Rex's leg?

A: A Dino Sore!

Q: Why did the rooster stop crossing the road?

A: He was too chicken!

Q: Where did the bee go to the toilet?

A: The BP station!

Q: Why wasn't the scarecrow very hungry?

A: He was already stuffed!

Q: What happens if you feed gun powder to chickens?

A: Egg-splosions!

Q: Why did the skeleton always miss the party?

A: He had no body to go with!

Q: What did the poodle say to the flea?

A: Stop bugging me!

Q: Where did the ghost go for his holiday?

A: Mali-booo!

Q: What did the traffic light say to the school bus?

A: Don't look, I'm changing!

Q: Why did the hummingbird always hum?

A: She forgot the words!

Q: Why did the tissue dance all night long?

A: It was full of boogey!

Q: Why did Darth Vader feel strange when Luke got him a gift for Christmas?

A: He felt his presents!

Q: How many skunks does it take to make your house smell bad?

A: A phew!

Q: Why was the spider hanging out on the computer?

A: He was making a website!

Q: If a lion ate a clown how would he feel?

A: A bit funny!

Q: What kind of flower is on your dad's face?

A: Tulips!

Q: What did the elephant say to her naughty children?

A: Tusk Tusk!

Q: What did the magic tractor do last Saturday?

A: Turned into a corn field!

Q: What did the thirsty vampire say to his friend as they went past the morgue?

A: Let's have a cool one!

Q: What did the dentist call her X-Rays?

A: Tooth Pics!

Q: What was the snake's favorite subject at snake school?

A: Hiss-story!

Q: What did the small light bulb say to the big light bulb?

A: Watts up?

Q: Who did the ghost go with to the movies?

A: His ghoul friend!

Q: What is Frankenstein's favorite play?
A: Romeo and Ghouliet!

Q: Why did the vampire have to go to the hospital?
A: He was coffin!

Q: How much does it cost when a pirate gets his ears pierced?
A: About a Buccaneer! (A buck an ear)

Q: When is it bad luck if a black cat follows you?
A: When you are a grey mouse!

Q: Why did the scarecrow get a big pay rise?

A: He was a leader in his field!

Q: What was in the scary ghost's nose?

A: Boooogers!

Q: How can you tell if a vampire is getting a cold?

A: By his loud coffin!

Q: What is a small dog's favorite type of pizza?

A: Pupparoni!

Q: Where do computers party all night?

A: The Disk O!

Q: How do birds learn to fly for the very first time?

A: They wing it!

Ridiculous
Jokes For Kids!

Q: What was the witch's favorite subject
at witch school?

A: Spelling!

Q: What kind of car did the cat drive to
work?

A: A Cattilac!

Q: How can you tell when a train is eating its lunch?

A: It goes choo-choo!

Q: Why did the golfer go to the dentist?

A: She had a hole in one!

Q: How do you know if a hippo has been living in your refrigerator?

A: There are footprints in the butter!

Q: If a butcher is 5 feet tall and has big feet what does he weigh?

A: Meat!

Q: What is the best time to go on a trampoline?

A: Springtime!

Q: Why didn't the girl want to kiss the vampire?

A: It's such a pain in the neck!

Q: Why was the fireman wearing red braces?

A: To keep up his trousers!

Q: What do you call a ship that has sunk and shivers on the bottom of the sea?

A: A nervous wreck!

Q: What did the math teacher who was constipated do?

A: He used a pencil to work it out!

Q: What washes up on really, really small beaches?

A: Microwaves!

Q: Why wouldn't the baby blueberry stop crying?

A: Her dad was in a jam!

Q: What do you call a bell that falls into the pool?

A: Wringing wet!

Q: Why was 6 really scared of 7?

A: 7, 8, 9!

Q: Why is it so cloudy and wet in England?

A: The queen always reigns there!

Q: What did the big raindrop say to the small raindrop?

A: Two's company but three's a cloud!

Q: How do small bees get to bee school?

A: On the school buzz!

Q: Why was the ocean so upset?

A: It had crabs on its bottom!

Q: What did the panda say on Halloween night?

A: Bam-BOOO!

Q: What has 4 legs, 1 tail and goes Ooom, Ooom?

A: A cow walking in reverse!

Q: What do you call a snowman who has been sunbaking for a week?

A: Water!

Q: Where is the witch's garage?

A: The broom closet!

Q: What do you get if you dive into the Red Sea?

A: Wet!

Q: Why did the strawberry look so sad?

A: It was a **blue berry!**

Q: Why didn't the mummies ever take time off?

A: They were scared to unwind!

Q: How does water stop flowing downhill?

A: It gets to the bottom!

Q: How do Australian oceans say G'day to each other?

A: They wave!

Q: Why did the witch itch?

A: She lost her W!

Q: Why did Humpty Dumpty love autumn so much?

A: He had a great fall!

Q: No matter how many times you try, which word is always spelt wrong?

A: Wrong!

Q: What happens if you cross a computer and a life guard?

A: You get a screensaver!

Q: What is the key to a great space party?

A: Always planet early!

Q: Which bet has never been won?

A: The alphabet!

Q: Which dinosaur spoke English and knew all the words?

A: The thesaurus!

Q: What was a better invention than the first telephone?
A: The second telephone!

Q: What has 4 legs, a trunk and wears sunglasses?
A: A mouse on holiday!

Q: What is the busiest time to go to the dentist?
A: Tooth hurty! (2.30)

Q: What did the thief get after he stole a calendar?
A: 12 months!

Q: What do you hear if you cross Bambi
with a ghost?

A: Bamboooo!

Q: What was the drummer's favorite vegetable?

A: Beets!

Q: Why was the detective duck given the key to the city?

A: He quacked the case!

Q: What would happen if you crossed a centipede with a parrot?

A: You get a walkie talkie!

Q: Why is the ocean always so clean?

A: Mermaids!

Q: Where do you find a dog with two ears, one tail but no legs?

A: Exactly where you left him!

Q: What was the alligator's favorite game?

A: Snap!

Q: What roads do ghosts like to haunt?
A: Dead ends!

Q: What did the Cinderella penguin wear to the ball?
A: Glass flippers!

Q: What is the best place for an elephant to store her luggage?
A: In her trunk!

Q: Why was the baker a millionaire?
A: He made heaps of dough!

Bonus Funny Jokes For Funny Kids!

Q: What is the correct name for a sleeping bull?

A: A bulldozer!

Q: Why did the cat jump up on the computer?

A: So she could catch the mouse!

Q: How long do Math Teachers live for?

A: Until their number is up!

Q: What do you call a bird that has escaped from its cage?

A: A Polygon! (Polly gone)

Q: What did the dinosaur eat after his tooth was pulled out?

A: The dentist!

Q: What happens if it's been raining cats and dogs?

A: You might step in a poodle!

Q: What is the name of the cat that lives at the hospital?

A: First aid kit!

Q: Why did the boy take 3 rolls of toilet paper to the birthday party?

A: He was a party pooper!

Q: Where do fish keep their spare cash?

A: The river bank!

Q: Where do all polar bears go to vote?
A: The North Poll!

Q: Why did the butterfly leave the dance?
A: It was a moth ball!

Q: Why did the boy pour hot water down a rabbit hole?
A: He wanted some hot cross bunnies!

Q: Why didn't the girl like the pizza joke?

A: It was way too cheesy!

Q: What did the toilet roll say to the toilet?

A: You're looking a bit flushed!

Q: What do you call a football playing cat?

A: Puss in boots!

Q: Why did the cows all go to Broadway?

A: To see the mooosicals!

Q: What do you call a lion that likes to wear top hats?

A: A dandy lion!

Q: What do you call an elephant that didn't have a bath for a year?

A: A smellyphant!

Q: What was the pirate's favorite subject at school?

A: Arrrrrt!

Q: Which puzzle makes you more angry the more you do it?

A: A Crossword puzzle!

Q: What time is it when an elephant sits on your lunch box?

A: Time to get a new lunch box!

Q: What is the quietest dog in the world?

A: A hush puppy!

Q: What did the tooth say to the dentist when he went to the movies?

A: Fill me in when you get back!

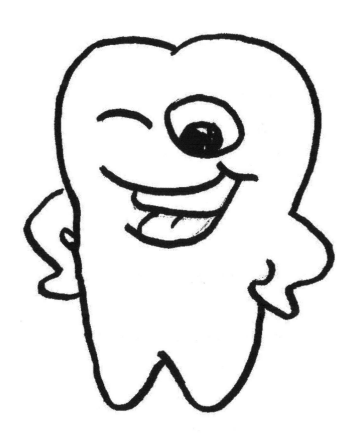

Q: What is even better than a talking dog?

A: A spelling bee!

Q: Why did the swimmer stop swimming?

A: The sea weed!

Q: Why did the orange fall asleep at work?

A: He ran out of juice!